Disney
PRINCESS

My Princess Collection

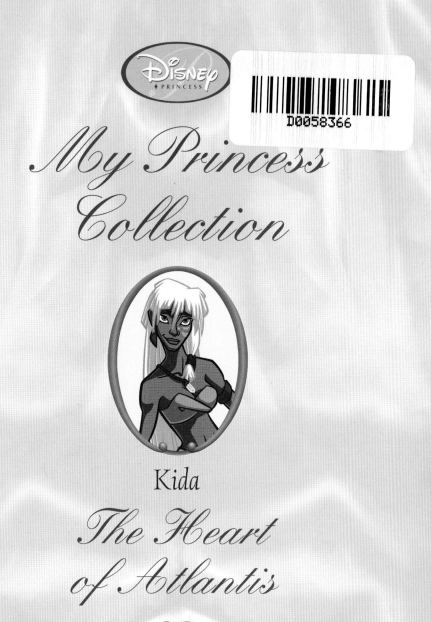

Kida

The Heart of Atlantis

Book Seven

Chapter One

My name is Kidagakash. Some people call me Kida. I am queen of Atlantis. But my story starts long before I became queen. It begins many thousands of years ago when I was a tiny child of just 600 or so years.

Our city, Atlantis, was in terrible danger. It was being destroyed by great forces. As I ran through the city with my father, the king, and my mother, the queen, the great Crystal suddenly appeared above us. The Crystal guards us and protects us in times of terrible distress. As our city was about to be destroyed due to our greedy ways, the Crystal decided to accept a sacrifice—someone of royal birth to save the city. It chose my mother.

I believe she was chosen not just because she was royal but also because she was good. When she was joined with the Crystal, she left me forever. I was terribly sad, but I knew that she had saved us all.

Soon, our city sank deep below the ocean and continued to exist in a bubble beneath the surface. We did not thrive, but we existed in peace . . . for a while.

Chapter Two

My father, King Kashekim Nedakh, was a wise and good ruler, but he did not tell us about our past. He did not let us know that we had caused our own downfall. Because of our greed, we had used our powers and special gifts to try to take over the world, rather than trying to cure diseases and help others.

My father did this to protect us. He was in terrible grief over the loss of my mother, and he did not want our people to suffer anymore. So, for years, he hid our own great skills from us.

We did not know that we could read and write; we did not know that we had flying vehicles and knowledge of great things, all of which could have helped us thrive. My father wanted his people to be ignorant . . . and safe.

Then one day, everything changed.

Chapter Three

It all began when a man named Milo Thatch and a group of explorers from the surface came to our world. We first saw them as they camped outside our city. We knew they were lost, but we also feared them. Who were these strangers? What did they want?

Soon, they found our hidden city. I was immediately intrigued by Milo Thatch. He was smart and funny. And he could answer many of my questions about life on the surface!

Milo Thatch was good to us. But his companions were greedy. They asked him to find out information about us. Milo didn't understand their greed. He just wanted to know us better.

As soon as I learned Milo could read Atlantean, I took him to my workshop.

"Here, let me show you something," I said. It was an ancient flying vehicle our ancestors had used before us. It had sat idle for hundreds of years because none of us could read the writing on its controls.

Milo read the instructions—and soon the flying machine came to life! We even went for a ride over the city. It was incredible!

After that, Milo helped me read the
ancient writings on the walls of our great
buildings that had long since sunk underwater.
He opened my mind to many things—both
about the world above us and about my own
world.

The others in Milo's group wanted to risk destroying our entire civilization so that they could steal the precious Crystal that provided our life force. They felt that they could make a great fortune by bringing the Crystal to the surface and selling it.

Little did we know that our lives were about to change forever.

Chapter Four

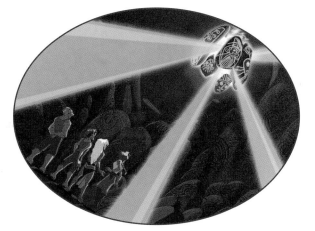

It started when the explorers' terrible leader, Commander Rourke, kidnapped me and brought me to the center of Atlantis to meet with the Crystal.

Overwhelmed, I saw the great kings of the past rise to protect the Crystal. I sank to my knees, with tears in my eyes. "Spirits of Atlantis, forgive us for defiling your chambers and bringing intruders into the land," I said in Atlantean.

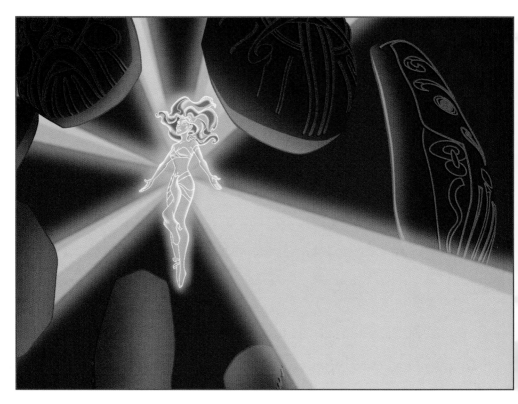

The Crystal sensed the danger, and I could feel its spirit inside me. At last I knew my time had come. The great kings of the past joined together and helped me unite with the Crystal, exactly as my mother had done thousands of years earlier.

But I was lucky. Milo Thatch convinced some of his companions to help him save Atlantis. They stood their ground against their evil leader, Commander Rourke.

When Rourke said, "Let's move, people," Milo's companions refused to budge.

Then Milo led them into a fierce battle
to save me. He showed them how to start
the ancient flying vehicles. Soon the entire
Atlantean armada took off after Rourke.

At last, it came down to Milo's battle
against Rourke. Milo alone was the one who
defeated the wicked man and saved my life.

Unfortunately, a great strain was put on the Crystal. In the end, my father lost his life. But my city was saved. And the great Crystal gave me back to my people, allowing me to float down into Milo Thatch's arms.

Chapter Five

When I awoke in Milo's arms, I was holding a tiny bracelet . . . from my mother. Her spirit existed in the Crystal. As I gazed at the bracelet and felt his arms around me, I felt grateful that I had met Milo Thatch.

Now I am queen of Atlantis. I wish to teach my people about their past, and try to tell them how to avoid the temptations of greed. I miss my father terribly, but now I know that my mother is watching over me . . . from her place inside the great Crystal. And Milo Thatch has decided to live here with us. He will help me rule Atlantis, and he will stay with me always, right by my side.